The Case of the Five Orange Pips

A Jamestown
Classic
adapted from
Arthur Conan Doyle

D1242316

Walter Pauk, Ph.D.
Professor of Education
Director, Reading-Study Center
Cornell University

Raymond Harris

Jamestown
Publishers

Providence
Rhode Island

The Case of the Five Orange Pips

Student Booklet, No.545

adapted from
Arthur Conan Doyle

Cover, Text Design by Stephen R. Anthony
Illustrations by Robert James Pailthorpe

Printed in the United States   AL
87 88 89 90 9 8 7 6 5 4 3

ISBN 0-89061-062-2

Contents

The Case of the Five Orange Pips

As I look over my notes and records of the many cases of Sherlock Holmes that have not yet been written, none presents such strange happenings as the case of the five orange pips. Let me begin by telling the story from my notes and memory.

It was late September, the season for high winds and heavy rains. On this special night, the wind hurled itself at our windows and doors, and howled in the chimney. It threw cloud after cloud of hard-balled rain at the fragile panes. And one couldn't help but wonder how much longer the windows could hold out against such primitive and tireless forces. Sherlock Holmes sat moodily at one side of the fireplace sorting his records of crime, while I, at the other side, was in the middle of a storm in one of Clark Russell's fine sea-stories. The storm outside and the storm in the story blended so perfectly that soon I did not know one from the other. But suddenly, I was brought back to reality.

"Why," said I, glancing up at Holmes, "that was surely the bell. Who would come tonight? Some friend of yours, perhaps?"

"Except yourself, I have none," he answered. "I do not encourage visitors."

"A client, then?"

"If so, it is a serious case. Nothing less would bring a man out on such a day and at such an hour. More likely, it is some friend of the landlady's."

Sherlock Holmes was wrong in his guess. For soon we heard a step in the hall, then a tap at the door. "Come in!" he called.

The man who entered was young—not over twenty-two. He was well groomed and trimly dressed. His dripping umbrella and his shining raincoat told of the fierce weather through which he had come. Holmes kindly took both and hung them on a hook to dry.

"I have come for advice."

"That is easily got," said Holmes.

"And help."

"That, is not always so easy," replied Holmes.

The youth continued, "Major Pendergast told me about you. He said that you could solve anything."

"He said too much," answered Holmes.

"That you are never beaten."

"I have been beaten four times—three times by men and once by a woman," was Holmes's thoughtful reply.

"But what is that compared to the number of your successes?"

"It is true that I have been generally successful."

"I hope then that you may be so with me."

"I beg that you will draw your chair up to the fire and give me some details of your case."

The young man pulled up his chair and pushed his wet feet towards the blaze.

"My name," said he, "is John Shaw. To give you the details of this awful business, I must go back to the very beginning.

"My grandfather had two sons—my Uncle Elias and my father Joseph. My father had a small but very successful factory at Coventry. When he finally sold it, he had more than enough to retire on. My Uncle Elias, however, sailed to America when he was a young man and became a planter in the South. He was reported to have done very well. At the time of the Civil War he fought in Jackson's army where he rose to be a colonel.

"When Lee laid down his arms, my uncle returned to his plantation. He remained there for four years. About 1870, he came back to England and bought some land in Sussex. He left America, he said, because he hated the carpet-bag government in his defeated state.

"My uncle was a quick-tempered man who kept to himself most of the time. During the day he worked in his garden, and in the evening he drank a great deal of whiskey and smoked cigars. He would see no one and did not want any friends, not even his own brother. He didn't, however, mind me. In fact, he liked me from the beginning. I was about twelve then. Actually, he begged my father to let me live with him, and he was very kind to me in his way. It was my job to deal with the servants and tradesmen, so that by the time I was sixteen, I was quite the master of the house.

"One day—it was in March, 1883— a letter with a foreign stamp lay upon the table in front of the colonel's plate. 'From Pondicherry, India!' said he as he took it up. 'What can this be?' He opened it hurriedly. Out jumped five little dried orange pips, which pattered down upon his plate. I began to laugh at this, but the laugh was struck from my lips at the sight of his face. His lip fell, his eyes stuck out, his skin paled, and he stared at the envelope which he still held in his shaking hand. 'K.K.K.!' he cried. And then, 'My God, my God, my sins have overtaken me!'"

" 'What is it, uncle?' I cried.

" 'Death,' said he. He rose from the table and went to his room. I sat there, shaking with horror. I picked up the envelope and saw, printed in red ink upon the inner flap, just above the gummed part, the letter K three times repeated. What could be the reason of his overpowering terror? As I entered the house, I met him coming down the stairs with a small brass box.

" 'They may do what they like, but I'll stop them still,' said he. 'Tell Mary that I shall want a fire in my room today, and send for Mr. Fordham, the lawyer.'

"When the lawyer arrived, I was asked to come into the room too. The fire was burning brightly, and in the grate there was a mass of black, fluffy ashes, as of burned paper, while the brass box stood open and empty beside it. As I looked around, I noticed that upon the lid of the box was printed the triple K which I had seen upon the envelope.

" 'I wish you, John,' said my uncle, 'to witness my will. I leave my estate to my brother, your father. He will, in turn, leave it to you. If you can enjoy it in peace, well and good!

If you find you cannot, take my advice, my boy, and leave it to your worst enemy. I am sorry to give you such a two-edged thing, but I can't say what turn things are going to take.'

"This incident, which started with one letter, made a deep impression on me. I thought about the five orange pips, but was unable to make anything of it. Yet, I could not shake off the feeling of heavy dread. As the weeks passed, I could see a change in my uncle. He drank more. When very drunk, he would suddenly burst out of the house and tear about the garden with a gun in his hand. He'd scream out that he was afraid of no man. When these hot fits were over, however, he would rush into the house and quickly bar the door. I have seen his face, even on a cold day, wet with sweat.

"Well, to make the story short, Mr. Holmes, there came a night when he rushed out but never came back. We found him face down in a little green-scummed pool. There was no sign of a struggle. The water was but two feet deep. The jury brought in a verdict of 'suicide.' But I, who knew him, knew how much he loved life. The matter passed, however, and my father took possession of the estate."

"One moment," Holmes interrupted, "your story is one of the most remarkable I ever heard. Let me have the date of the letter, and the date of your uncle's death."

"The letter arrived on March 10, 1883. His death was seven weeks later, upon the night of May 2d."

"Thank you. Please go on," said Sherlock Holmes.

"When my father took over the estate, we examined the attic. There we found the brass box. It was empty, of course. The papers had been burned. On the inside of the cover was pasted a slip of paper, with the letters K.K.K. on it. And under the letters were written the words: 'Secret Records and Reports.' These, we felt, were the kinds of papers that had been burned.

"Well, it was about nine months later that my father came to live at the estate. All went well until the January of 1885. On the fourth day of the month I heard my father give a sharp cry of surprise as we sat together at breakfast. There he was, sitting with an envelope in one hand and five dried orange pips in the other. He had always laughed at my story about the colonel. But, now, he looked pale and very frightened when the same thing happened to him.

" 'What on earth does this mean, John?' he cried.

"My heart had turned to lead. 'It is the K.K.K.,' said I.

"He looked inside the envelope and read these words.

" 'Put the papers on the sundial. ' "

" 'What papers? What sundial?' he asked.

" 'The sundial in the garden. There is no other,' said I; 'but the papers must be those that have been burned.'

"My father then tried to pass the letter off as a joke. I noticed that the letter was posted at Dundee. He would not let me make a report of this to the police. He said, 'I'd be laughed at.' After that, I went about with a heart full of fear.

"On the third day after the letter, my father went to visit an old friend of his in the next town. I was glad that he should get away from danger for a time. In that, however, I was wrong. On the second day of his visit I received a telegram telling me to come at once. My father had fallen into one of the deep chalk-pits in that area. He was found lying at the bottom with a crushed skull. I hurried to him, but he died without regaining consciousness. The jury brought in a verdict of 'death from accidental causes.' Again, the police found no signs of violence. But I was certain that some devilish plot had been woven around him.

"It was in January, 1885, that my poor father met his death. Two years and eight months have gone by. I had begun to hope that this curse had passed away from the family. But I had begun to take comfort too soon. Yesterday morning the blow fell in the very same way on me."

The young man took an envelope from his coat. He held it over the table and shook it. Out dropped five little dried orange pips.

"This is the envelope," he said. "The postmark is London. Inside are the same letters: 'K.K.K.'; and then 'Put the papers on the sundial.' "

"What have you done?" asked Holmes.

"Nothing."

"Nothing?"

"To tell the truth"—he sank his face into his thin, white hands—"I have felt helpless. I have felt like one of those poor rabbits when a snake is about to strike."

"Tut! tut!" said Sherlock Holmes. "You must act, or you are lost. There is no time for such feelings."

"I have seen the police."

"Ah!"

"But they listened to my story with a smile."

Holmes shook his fists in the air.

"They have, however, allowed me a policeman."

"Has he come with you tonight?"

"No. His orders were to stay in the house."

Again Holmes waved his hands in the air.

"Why did you not come to me at once?"

"I did not know. It was only today that I spoke to Major Pendergast.

"It is really two days since you had the letter. We should have acted before this."

"Yes, but what shall I do?"

"There is but one thing to do. It must be done at once. You must take that brass box which you have described. Then, you must put into it a note to say that all of the papers were burned by your uncle. You must say this in such words as will convince them that you are telling the truth. Having done this, you must at once put the box out on the sundial, as directed. Do you understand?"

"Yes, I do."

"Do not think of revenge. The first act is to remove the present danger which threatens you."

"I thank you," said the young man, rising and pulling on his raincoat and taking his umbrella. "You have given me fresh life and hope. I shall certainly do as you say."

"Do not lose an instant. And, above all, take care of yourself. There is no question that a very real danger hangs over your head. How do you go back?"

"By train from Waterloo Station."

"It is not yet nine. The streets will be crowded, so I trust that you may be in safety. And yet you cannot guard yourself too closely."

"I am armed."

"That is well. Tomorrow I shall set to work on your case."

Outside the wind still screamed and the rain dashed against the windows. This strange, wild story seemed to have come to us from amid the mad elements—blown in upon us like a sheet of seaweed in a storm—and now to have been washed back into the angry sea by the tide.

Sherlock Holmes sat for some time in silence. His head was sunk forward and his eyes staring at the red glow of the fire. Then he lit his pipe, and leaning back in his chair, he watched the blue smoke rings as they chased each other up to the ceiling.

"I think, Watson," he remarked at last, "that of all our cases we have had none more fantastic than this. John Shaw is walking amid great danger."

"But have you," I asked, "formed any clear idea as to what these dangers are?"

"There can be no question as to their nature," he answered.

"Then what are they? Who is this K.K.K., and why does he pursue this unhappy family?"

Sherlock Holmes closed his eyes and placed his elbows upon the arms of his chair. Pressing his finger-tips together, he said, "I could give you the answer in my own words, but to make the answer more official, I should like to read it to you. Kindly hand me down the letter K of the *American Encyclopedia*. Thank you. But first, let us think through the case as we now have it, and see what may be deduced from it. In the first place, we may start with a strong guess that Colonel Shaw had some very powerful reason for leaving America. Men of his age do not change all their habits so suddenly. Very few people would willingly exchange the charming climate of the South for the lonely life on an English farm. His strong desire to be alone in England makes me believe that he was in fear of someone or something. So we may assume that this fear drove him from America. As to what it was he feared, we can only guess by going back to the letters that were received by the colonel, by Joseph Shaw, and now by John Shaw. Did you notice the postmarks of those letters?"

"The first was from Pondicherry, India, the second from Dundee in Scotland, and the third from London."

"What do you deduce from that?"

"They are all seaports. That the writer was on board a ship."

"Excellent. We already have a clue. And now let us consider another point. In the case of Pondicherry, India, there were seven weeks between the time the letter was received and death. In Dundee—Scotland is not so far away—it was only three or four days. Does that mean anything?"

"The killers, when they left India, had more miles to travel," said I.

"But, my dear Watson," Holmes came right back, "the letter also had to come over those same miles."

"Then I do not see the point," I said.

"My guess is that the vessel in which the man or men are in is a sailing ship. It looks as if they always sent their warning before them when starting upon their mission. I think that those seven weeks represent the difference between the mail-boat which brought the letter and the sailing vessel which brought the writer."

"It is possible," answered Watson.

"Now you can see why I urged young John Shaw to hurry. The blow has always come at the end of the time which it would take the senders to travel the distance. But this last letter comes from London, and therefore we cannot count upon delay."

"Good God!" I cried. "What do these killers want?"

"The papers which Colonel Shaw originally had are of great importance to the man or men in the sailing ship. I think that it is quite clear that there must be more than one man. A single man could not have carried out two deaths in such a way as to fool a coroner's jury. In this way, you see, the letters K.K.K. do not stand for any person. Rather, they stand for a society."

"But of what society?"

"Have you never—" said Sherlock Holmes, bending forward and sinking in his voice—"have you never heard of the Ku Klux Klan?"

"I never have."

Holmes turned the pages of the encyclopedia. "Here it is," said he presently—"I'll read the first part:"

Ku Klux Klan. The name is made up of the sound produced by the cocking of a rifle. This terrible secret society was formed by some ex-Confederate soldiers in the Southern states after the Civil War. Its power was used for political purposes, chiefly for terrorizing and murdering and driving from the country those who were opposed to its views. Its outrages were usually preceded by a warning sent to a marked man. For some years the organization grew in spite of the efforts of the United States government. Eventually, in the year 1869, the movement rather suddenly collapsed, although there have been minor outbreaks since then."

"You will notice," said Holmes, "that the sudden breaking up of the society was at the exact time that Colonel Shaw left America. You see, he had their secret papers. You can understand how these papers and records may involve some of the most important men in the South. There are many, no doubt, who will not sleep easy at night until all these papers are found and brought back. So I believe the only chance young Shaw has is to do what I told him. But there's nothing more can be done tonight. Therefore, let us try for the moment to forget the miserable weather and the more miserable ways of our fellowmen."

It had cleared by morning, and the sun was shining. Sherlock Holmes was already at breakfast when I came down.

"You will excuse me for not waiting for you," said he. "I have a very busy day before me."

"What steps will you take?" I asked.

"I shall start with the City. Just ring the bell and the maid will bring your coffee."

As I waited, I lifted the unopened newspaper from the table. My eye was drawn to a heading which sent a chill to my heart.

"Holmes," I cried, "you are too late."

"Ah!" said he, laying down his cup. "I feared as much. How was it done?" He spoke calmly, but I could see that he was deeply moved.

"The heading is 'Tragedy Near Waterloo Bridge.' Here is the account.

"Between nine and ten last night, Constable Cook, on duty near Waterloo Bridge, heard a cry for help and a splash in the water. The night, however, was dark and stormy. It was impossible to effect the rescue. The water-police finally found the body. An envelope found on the body identified the gentleman as John Shaw. It appears that he may have been hurrying to catch the last train from Waterloo Station. In his haste and the darkness, he missed his path and walked over the edge of a small dock for river steamboats. There were no traces of violence. There can be no doubt that the dead man had been the victim of an accident."

We sat in silence for some minutes. Holmes was more depressed and shaken than I had ever seen him.

At last he said, "That he should come to me for help, and that I should send him away to his death!" He sprang from his chair and paced about the room. His sallow cheeks were flushed and he closed and opened his long thin hands nervously.

"They must be clever devils," he said at last. "How could they have trapped him down there? The dock is not on the direct line to the station. The bridge, no doubt, was too crowded, even on such a night, for their purpose. Excuse me, Watson, I am going out now!"

It was late in the evening before I returned to Baker Street. Sherlock Holmes had not come back yet. It was nearly ten o'clock before he entered, looking pale and worn.

"Have you had any success?" I asked.

Silently, he took a large sheet of paper from his pocket, all covered with dates and names.

"I have spent the whole day," said he, "over at Lloyd's searching the records and files of every ship that docked at Pondicherry in January and February of 1883. Of the many, only one, the *Lone Star,* caught my eye because that is a name given to one of the states of the Union. Texas, I think. So I knew it was American."

"What then?"

"Then I searched the Dundee records. I found that the *Lone Star* was there in January, '85."

"Yes?"

"I then checked the ships presently in the Port of London. As I expected, I saw that the *Lone Star* had arrived here last week. I rushed to the Albert Dock but found that she had left down the river by the early tide this very morning. I found out, too, that the ship is in charge of a Captain James Calhoun. He and the two mates are the only native-born Americans on the ship. The others are hired deck hands from other countries. I know, also, that these three were away from the ship last night. There are two dock workers will swear to that. At this moment the ship is heading home for Savannah.

"What will you do now?"

"I have done everything I possibly could. Their doom, however, is sealed. I hurried over to Scotland Yard and fortunately Lestrade was there. An officer sent a wire to Savannah. The police there will pick up the men and send them back to us under guard to stand trial for murder. I will do everything in my power to help avenge the death of young John Shaw."

There is always a flaw, however, in the best laid plans of men. Very long and very harsh were the autumn storms that year. We waited long for news of the *Lone Star,* but none ever reached us. We did at last hear that somewhere far out in the Atlantic the shattered mast of a ship was seen floating on a wave. Carved on the mast were the letters "L.S." And that is all that we shall ever know of the fate of the *Lone Star.*

Glossary

Glossary

The Case of the Five Orange Pips
A Glossary of Words and Expressions

Key Concepts

Key Concepts

The Case of the Five Orange Pips
Understanding Key Concepts—Examining Values

These are short passages taken from the story, followed by three questions. In every case, question A can be answered without knowing the story and may be used for warm-up discussions.

Questions B and C should be kept in mind, while listening to the story or reading it, for discussion later. Answers to the A questions may also be reviewed at this time.

1. Spending a quiet evening at home, Sherlock Holmes was working on his records of crime, and Dr. Watson was reading a book (page 9):

> But suddenly, I was brought back to reality.
> "Why," said I, glancing up at Holmes, "that was surely the bell. Who would come tonight? Some friend of yours, perhaps?"
> "Except yourself, I have none," he answered. "I do not encourage visitors."

A. Would you judge that Sherlock Holmes is an unfriendly man? How do you feel about having people leave you alone?

B. John Shaw's uncle, Colonel Shaw, did not want any friends either. Were the colonel's and Sherlock Holmes's reasons similar?

C. Find a passage in the story to show Sherlock Holmes's feelings (warm or unwarm) toward people.

2. John Shaw, a young man of about 22, had just come to Sherlock Holmes's apartment (page 9):

> "I have come for advice."
> "That is easily got," said Holmes.
> "And help."
> "That, is not always so easy," replied Holmes.

A. Why is it easier to give advice than help? Do you usually get more advice than help? Why?

B. What advice did Sherlock Holmes give to John Shaw?

C. Did the advice given turn out to be of help? Explain your opinion.

3. Colonel Shaw, an Englishman by birth, fought in the American Civil War for the South. After the war he returned to England (page 10):

> He left America, he said, because he hated the carpet-bag government in his defeated state.

A. What would you do if you hated your state government?

B. Can you think of any recent political policy which caused many young Americans to leave the country?

C. What do you think was the real reason for Colonel Shaw's leaving America?

4. John Shaw's father received a threatening letter (page 13):

> "My father then tried to pass the letter off as a joke. I noticed that the letter was posted at Dundee. He would not let me make a report of this to the police. He said, 'I'd be laughed at.'

    A. What sorts of things do *you not do* because you might be laughed at?

    B. Was the father right in not reporting this letter to the police? Explain your opinion.

    C. Would it have made a difference if the report had been made? Why?

5. Young John Shaw is faced with a problem. He had received the same kind of threatening letter that had come just before the deaths of his uncle and father (page 14):

> "What have you done?" asked Holmes.
> "Nothing."
> "Nothing?"
> "To tell the truth" —he sank his face into his thin, white hands— "I have felt helpless. I have felt like one of those poor rabbits when a snake is about to strike."

A. Have you ever faced a situation in which you did nothing because everything seemed hopeless? Is there ever a situation in which absolutely nothing can be done?

B. Was John Shaw's situation as hopeless as he made it out to be?

C. What action should John Shaw have taken? What could he have done to save himself?

Comprehension Questions

Comprehension Questions

The Case of the Five Orange Pips
How Well Did You Understand the Story?

Choose the letter which best answers each question.

1. On the night that John Shaw came to Sherlock Holmes for help, it was
   - a. foggy.
   - b. hailing.
   - c. raining.
   - d. snowing.

2. John Shaw's uncle, Colonel Shaw, was
   - a. an easy-going man.
   - b. a quick-tempered man.
   - c. a very sociable man.
   - d. a non-smoking man.

3. The letter from Pondicherry, India, contained
   - a. five poisonous seeds.
   - b. five orange-colored pills.
   - c. five pills of snake poison.
   - d. five dried orange pips.

4. The papers in the brass box were
   - a. burned by Colonel Shaw.
   - b. turned over to the lawyer.
   - c. given to young John Shaw.
   - d. locked again in the brass box.

5. Colonel Shaw was found dead
   - a. with a bullet hole behind the ear.
   - b. with his face in a pool of water.
   - c. at the bottom of a pit.
   - d. in the water under Waterloo Bridge.

6. After receiving the letter, John Shaw's father died. The jury said his death was from
   a. suicide.
   b. murder.
   c. accidental causes.
   d. manslaughter.

7. Young John Shaw's letter was postmarked in
   a. London.   c. Dundee.
   b. Pondicherry.   d. Savannah.

8. Sherlock Holmes's advice to John Shaw was to place the brass box on the sundial with
   a. the original papers in it.
   b. a note of explanation in it.
   c. a large sum of money in it.
   d. five pips of solid gold.

9. The papers which Colonel Shaw originally had were connected with
   a. American politics.
   b. the secret K.K.K. society.
   c. military secrets of the Civil War.
   d. names of men who deserted the army.

10. The sailing ship, the *Lone Star*, most probably
    a. escaped to Texas.
    b. sailed back to Pondicherry.
    c. survived the heavy storm.
    d. sank during a heavy storm.

Discussion Starters

The Case of the Five Orange Pips
Discussion Starters

1. The whole story has the atmosphere of a storm about it. Describe how you feel at night when there's a storm raging outside. What do you expect when there is a storm raging in a story?

2. Why do you think John Shaw's uncle was quick-tempered? Are quick-tempered people born that way, or do they become quick-tempered by what happens to them in life?

3. Are people who drink a great deal usually sociable? Why do some people drink too much? Does drinking help solve problems or does it create problems?

4. Do the sins an individual commits usually catch up with him? Can a person ever get away clean after doing something he knows is wrong?

5. Some people say that Colonel Shaw *deserved* to die. What is your opinion of this?

6. John Shaw said that his father always laughed at the story of the Colonel and the orange pips. But when it happened to him, he looked pale and very frightened. Why are things different when they happen to you, rather than to someone else?

7. Do you think it was wise for Sherlock Holmes to permit John Shaw to go home alone? How much responsibility did Sherlock Holmes take on when he agreed to take the case? How would you have handled things?

8. What do you know about the Ku Klux Klan? Did the ex-confederates have a right to form such an organization? What is your opinion of the first Klans? What do you think of the modern-day Ku Klux Klan?

9. Sherlock Holmes reasoned that John Shaw was trapped into going under the bridge where he was killed. How do you think this might have happened?

10. The men on the *Lone Star* probably drowned at sea. Does this even the score? Was justice done? Does their drowning make up for the deaths of the three Shaws? Why do you think the author ended the story this way instead of having the murderers caught and brought to justice?